THIS BOOK BELONGS TO

_____

WITH LOVE FROM

_____

For my children Natasha, Lev, and Maksim.
I'm so proud of all your hard work and perseverance in music
and hockey. Pass these lessons in love on to your children.
–XO Love, Mama Bear

For my beloved "little/big bear" son, Felix,
who fulfills his every dream with passion
and so much determination.
So proud of you.
–CB

ZONDERKIDZ

Candace Center Stage

Copyright © 2018 by Candache, Inc.
Illustrations © 2018 by Christine Battuz

This book is also available as a Zondervan ebook.

Requests for information should be addressed to:

Zonderkidz, 3900 Sparks Dr. SE, Grand Rapids, Michigan 49546

ISBN 978-0-310-76287-4

Design: Cindy Davis

Printed in China

18 19 20 21 /DSC/ 23 22 21 20 19 18 17 16 15 14 13 12 11 10 9 8 7 6 5 4 3 2 1

CandaCe CenTer STage

WRITTEN BY CANDACE CAMERON BURE

ILLUSTRATED BY CHRISTINE BATTUZ

ZONDERkidz

Candace loved to dance. She whirled and twirled. She twisted and turned.

Fun!

And even though
her mother was
always telling her
not to, she swung
on chandeliers,

dangled from doorways,

Funner!

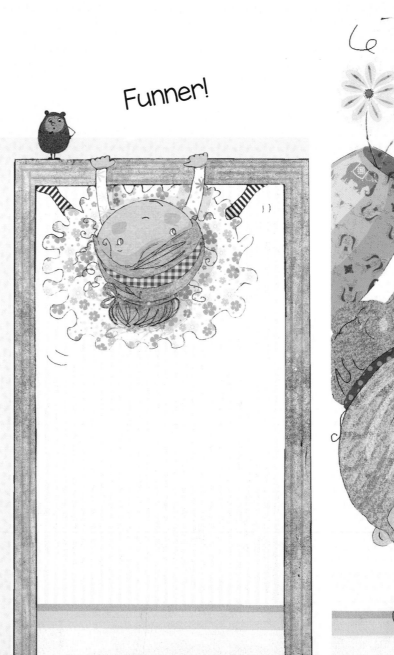

and leapt from her bed to
her dresser to the window
seat with her pet hamster, Harry.

Funnest!

No matter where she went, Candace danced.

So her mother signed her up for ballet lessons.

Candace couldn't wait for the day she'd dance on stage in front of a real audience that clapped and cheered and handed her big, beautiful bouquets of flowers.

On the day of her first ballet lesson,
Candace wore a special costume
and brought her own music.

She even brought Harry along.

I'm a ballerina and so is Harry.

But Candace quickly realized ballet wasn't as easy as she thought.

1st position,
2nd position,
3rd position.

My position!

Miss Grace tried to teach
Candace the proper positions.

But Candace was more
interested in shakes and shimmies
than pliés and relevés.

Sophie Rose, the best ballerina in the class, showed Candace how to do an arabesque.

Just do what I do.

Candace tried, but she just didn't move like the other ballerinas.

O

1

?

O

100

Thanks, Harry.

Candace told her mother ballet wasn't for her.

Candace's mother told her to stick with it.

One day in class, Miss Grace told the ballerinas there would be a recital.

Week after week, the ballerinas worked hard to learn the steps of the dance.

Candace worked hard too.

But as the recital drew near,
Candace still couldn't do all of the steps.

Sophie Rose had a talk with Candace.

If you don't learn the dance, you're going to ruin the show!

Take her away!

Candace feared Sophie Rose might be right.

So she did her very best . . . working harder than ever to make sure she was ready.

But on show night, Candace didn't feel ready. Her tutu was tailored, her bun was beautiful, but her tummy was a rumbly mess. There were so many people. Such bright lights …

And Sophie Rose!

Candace told Sophie Rose she was scared.

Sophie Rose told Candace real ballerinas don't get scared.

When it was their turn to dance, Candace followed Sophie Rose and the other dancers onto the stage. The lights went on.

Miss Grace cued the dancers to begin.

But when the music started, no one moved.

Candace looked at Sophie Rose who stood there like a statue.
Candace suddenly realized real ballerinas do get scared. *Even Sophie Rose!*

Then Candace had an idea. She took Sophie Rose's hand.

Then Sophie Rose
took Dilini's hand . . .
who took Helen
Elaine's hand . . . until
all the ballerinas
were holding hands.

Then Candace began to dance. She whirled and twirled. She shook and shimmied.
And with big smiles on their faces, all the ballerinas danced along with her.

Even Harry joined in!

When the song ended, Miss Grace motioned to the ballerinas to get back into line.

She started the music again. This time they performed the steps all together, exactly like they'd rehearsed.

When they finished, the audience clapped and cheered.
And the girls thanked Candace, who showed them anything's possible
if you work hard and have the courage to be yourself.

And Candace got a big, beautiful bouquet. Just like she always dreamed she would.

Dear Reader,

I hope you enjoyed *Candace Center Stage*!

This book is very personal to me as I've been acting in front of cameras since I was five years old. While I've played a lot of roles in my lifetime, you might know me best as my character D.J. Tanner on the TV shows *Full House* and *Fuller House*. And one of my dreams came true when I was asked to dance and compete on *Dancing with the Stars*, which inspired this book. I'm also an author, producer, wife, and mother of three and I couldn't imagine my life without playing every one of these roles.

I have been very fortunate to be able to do what I love and follow my passion for performing. Still, pursing my dreams hasn't always been easy. Not by a long shot! Like everyone else, I've had to deal with doubts, disappointments, and failures. It's taken hard work, patience, dedication, and a whole lot of faith to push my way through ... but I did it!

I hope this book inspires you. I hope it encourages you to pursue your dreams with perseverance. As I always say, "Dream big, pray harder." Believe, be true to yourself, and who knows what wonderful roles will come your way!

Lots of love,
Candace